# CHRISTMAS SWITCHEROO

**Christmas Switcheroo**

Story by **Tuula Pere**
Illustrations by **Outi Rautkallio**
Layout by **Peter Stone**
English translation by **Päivi Vuoriaro**
Edited in English by **Susan Korman**

ISBN 978-952-357-328-4 (Hardcover)
ISBN 978-952-357-329-1 (Paperback)
ISBN 978-952-357-330-7 (ePub)
Third re-illustrated edition

Copyright © 2014-2021 Tuula Pere and Wickwick Ltd

Published 2021 by Wickwick Ltd
Helsinki, Finland

Originally published in Finland by Wickwick Ltd in 2014
Finnish "Kummat lahjat", ISBN 978-952-5878-13-4 (Hardcover)
English "Christmas Switcheroo", ISBN 978-952-5878-22-6 (Hardcover)

Wickwick books are available at special discounts when purchased in quantity for premiums and promotions as well as fundraising or educational use. Special editions can also be created to specification. For details, contact specialsales@wickwick.fi.

# CHRISTMAS SWITCHEROO

TUULA PERE · OUTI RAUTKALLIO

Children's Books from the Heart

Christmas was a holiday that the Perkson family took very seriously. Preparations began well before the first snow. Mom, in particular, adored Christmas. During summer and fall, she would grow greens and dry berries for decorations.

"These will make great Christmas wreaths," Mom said, spreading her treasures all over the dining table.

2

The rest of the family was not that excited about wreaths. Or about the fact that, from October to December, the dining room table would be heaped with Mom's supplies for Christmas crafts.

But the family did enjoy listening to Christmas carols and eating gingerbread cookies even before all the leaves had fallen off the trees.

3

4

Meanwhile Dad was fiddling with electric gadgets for Christmas. He put up the Christmas lights, invented a heater for the bird feeder, and repaired the battery-operated elf that sang Christmas carols. If you clapped your hands together, the elf started singing loudly and jiggling itself wildly.

Every year, Dad bought more and more Christmas lights. He spent many evenings tinkering with them and changing the bulbs.

"I sure hope the fuses don't blow this year!" he said.

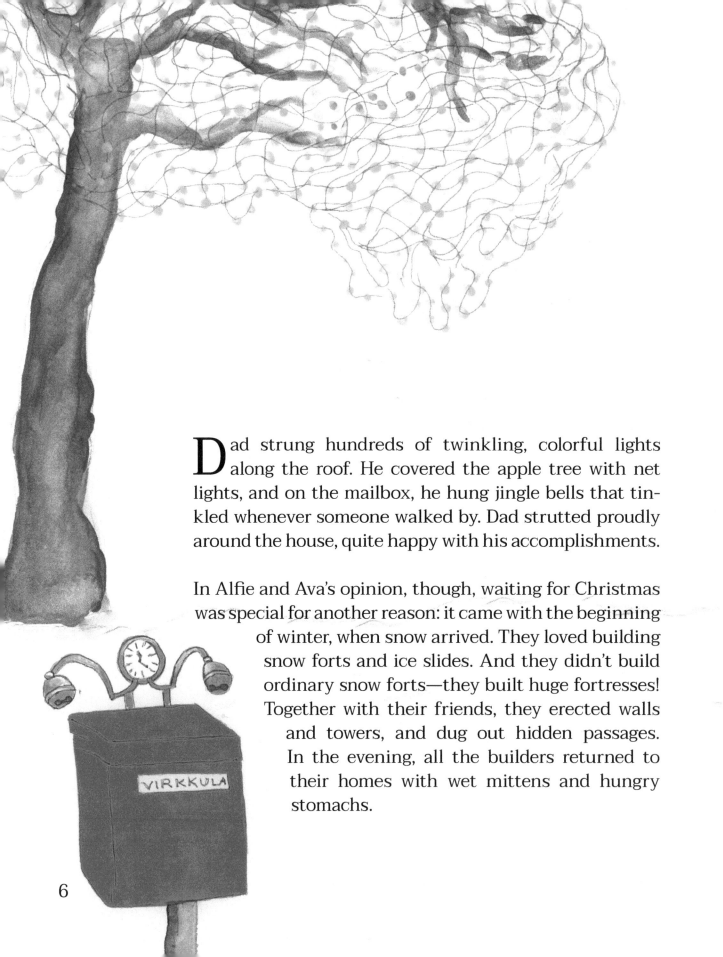

Dad strung hundreds of twinkling, colorful lights along the roof. He covered the apple tree with net lights, and on the mailbox, he hung jingle bells that tinkled whenever someone walked by. Dad strutted proudly around the house, quite happy with his accomplishments.

In Alfie and Ava's opinion, though, waiting for Christmas was special for another reason: it came with the beginning of winter, when snow arrived. They loved building snow forts and ice slides. And they didn't build ordinary snow forts—they built huge fortresses! Together with their friends, they erected walls and towers, and dug out hidden passages. In the evening, all the builders returned to their homes with wet mittens and hungry stomachs.

6

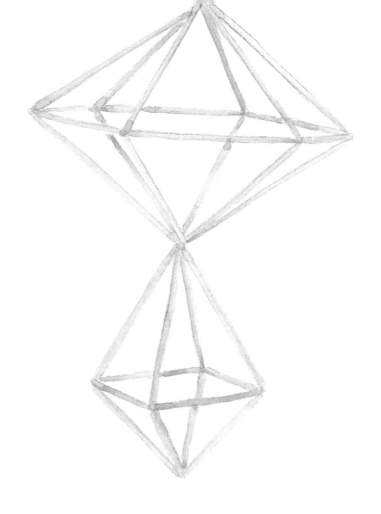

Mom was very good at arts and crafts. She had taken at least a dozen different sewing courses. She knew how to crochet, make lace, knit, quilt, and embroider. This year Mom had decided to crochet pretty covers for bottles. She was sure that all their relatives would love them. The coffee table was filled with balls of yarn in different colors.

"I just love waiting for Christmas." Mom sighed contently as she crocheted.

One night the smell of gingerbread filled the Perksons' house. The family sat down together to make a list of presents that they still needed to buy.

"We need four more presents," Dad said. "We still need gifts for Uncle Eddie, Cousin Scott, and Aunt Trudy. Plus, we need something for your godmother, Mildred."

"Let's surprise them with some cool gifts," Ava said.

Alfie grinned. "Yes!"

The family talked first about what to get Uncle Eddie. Their uncle had studied birds for so long he had begun to resemble an owl himself. The patterns on his favorite jacket looked just like an owl's plumage.

Mom often said Uncle Eddie was such a scatterbrain he even forgot his own name sometimes. The children never believed that, though. After all, Uncle Eddie could remember the names of all the birds—in Latin!

Uncle Eddie also recognized all the birds, even with his eyes closed. He knew them by their songs.

"Let's get Eddie a pet bird," Alfie said.

"What about a parrot?" Ava said.

"What a good idea," Mom said. "I bet Eddie can teach it to talk!"

11

The children's godmother, Mildred, was Mom's best friend. Or so it seemed to the children because Mom was on the phone with her all the time! The children had seen pictures of Mom and Mildred as little girls. Back then, they'd looked almost alike. But now they looked quite different.

Mom liked to say that Mildred had become a "visual artist," while she herself had become an "artist of life." Mildred had pitch-black hair with bangs as straight as an arrow, while Mom's hair was red with wild curls.

Everything in Mildred's house was black and white, and neatly organized. The Perksons' house meanwhile was filled with colors, stuff, and noise. Mildred sometimes said her head got dizzy in the commotion of the Perksons' house.

"What on earth can we get Mildred this Christmas?" Mom wondered aloud. "She doesn't want any more stuff."

"Let's get her another one of those artist's coats with colorful pockets," Dad suggested. "It's been at least five years since we gave her the last one."

"Who's next?" Alfie asked.

"Scott," Ava replied.

Ava and Alfie thought their cousin had become rather odd lately. He never wanted to build a snow fort or chat with the rest of the family anymore. Instead, all he wanted to do was sit in his room with his headphones on.

"It's nothing dangerous," Mom had reassured Ava and Alfie. "He's just entering the teenage years."

Ava and Alfie didn't quite understand.

"I never want to enter that age," Alfie declared. "Scott has become such a bore."

"Don't worry. It will pass," Mom reassured him.

"Let's get Scott an electric drum set," Dad said, getting excited. "I would have loved that as a teenager."

Aunt Trudy's gift was next. She was a tough cookie. She had strong opinions on everything under the sun, and she didn't shy away from sharing them.

"Nothing ever changes in that head of yours," Dad had once snapped at his aunt. "Not even those curly bangs!"

Luckily, their squabble had been over quickly. In the end, Dad and Aunt Trudy got along very well. There was no changing her opinion that the coffee maker and washing machine were the best technologies ever invented. So Dad knew he had no hope of getting his aunt excited about his own devices and inventions.

"I bet Aunt Trudy would like a curling iron," Mom said. "With it, she could curl her bangs in no time at all."

It was time to go shopping. Dad attached the trailer to the car.

Mom laughed. "What do we need the trailer for?" she asked. "We only need four more presents!"

"This morning I spotted an ad for a heated carport. I figured it would make a nice present for the whole family," Dad explained.

The children glanced at each other and grinned. How typical of Dad! they thought. Last Christmas the family present had been an automatic water-throwing machine for their sauna. It had broken down during its first use. They'd all had to rush out of the sauna when the machine wouldn't stop throwing water over the stones!

The town was very busy. It seemed as if everyone had decided to do Christmas shopping at the same time. The parking garage was packed.

With beads of sweat on his forehead, Dad drove around, looking for a parking space big enough for the car and the trailer. At last, he found one, and the family headed out to the shops. Mom and Dad decided to go to the big department store, while the children headed for the promenade and the Christmas market.

There was a small café along the promenade. It sold the most delicious hot cocoa in the world. The children happily sipped their chocolate drinks while admiring the treats in a glass display case.

"After you've wiped that cocoa moustache off your face, we could go to the library," Ava suggested to Alfie.

The library was the children's favorite spot in town. They always found fascinating books in the children's corner.

This time, however, they didn't borrow any books—there was a Christmas crafts program going on. In no time, Alfie and Ava had their own paper stars to take home and tape to a window.

"Let's just stay here for a while," Ava whispered, content.

Alfie nodded. "It's so quiet here—no shoppers and no crowds!"

"Too bad Mom and Dad are too busy to enjoy it too," Ava said with a sigh.

As Christmas drew nearer, the atmosphere in the Perksons' household grew tenser. As many as three trays of gingerbread had burned already, and Mom's home-made candles had turned out oddly colored and slanted.

Mom was getting upset. "How will I get everything finished in time?" she moaned. "I still need to wrap and mail our presents to all the relatives."

"We can help," the children promised.

"While you make the gingerbread houses, we'll wrap the packages," Alfie said.

Ava nodded. "We'll wrap neatly, and write the address labels in beautiful handwriting."

Mom looked relieved. "Thank you, kids," she said. "Here are the address labels and there are the presents. Please be careful."

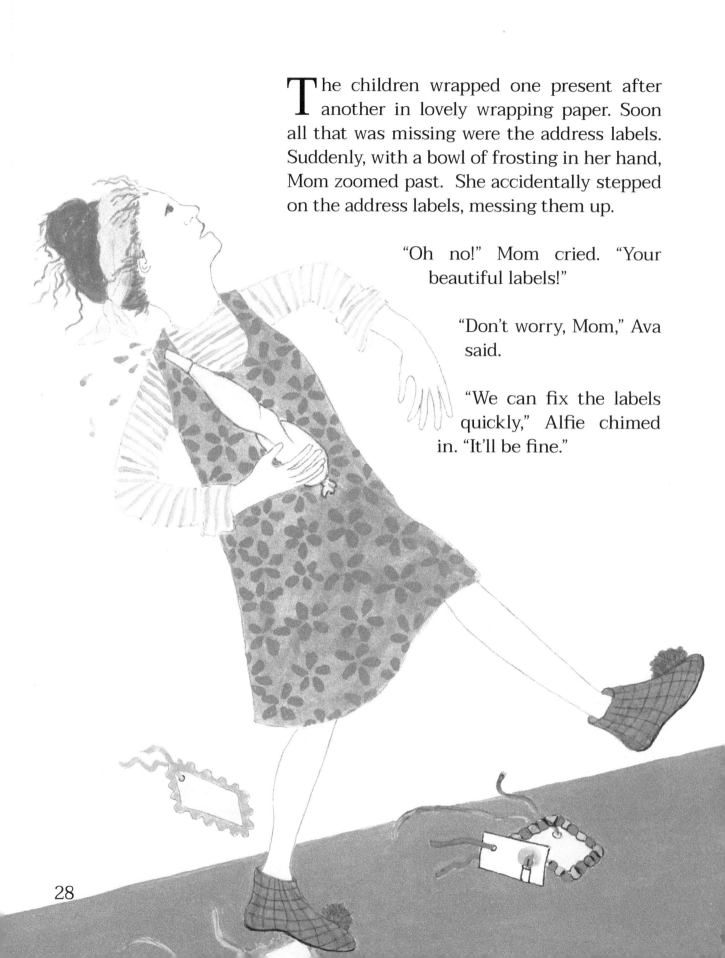

The children wrapped one present after another in lovely wrapping paper. Soon all that was missing were the address labels. Suddenly, with a bowl of frosting in her hand, Mom zoomed past. She accidentally stepped on the address labels, messing them up.

"Oh no!" Mom cried. "Your beautiful labels!"

"Don't worry, Mom," Ava said.

"We can fix the labels quickly," Alfie chimed in. "It'll be fine."

The children got back to work, rewriting the labels and attaching them to the packages. They worked quickly, before Mom could get upset again.

Later Dad looked at the packages. "To Uncle Eddie, Mildred, Scott, and Aunt Trudy," he read aloud. Then he grinned at the kids. "Great job. Tomorrow we'll go to the post office together."

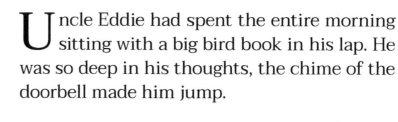

Uncle Eddie had spent the entire morning sitting with a big bird book in his lap. He was so deep in his thoughts, the chime of the doorbell made him jump.

"What's that? What's happening? Oh, it's only the doorbell," Uncle Eddie mumbled.

U ncle Eddie had no difficulty staying quiet and still for hours on end when bird watching. But with presents, he had no patience whatsoever!

"A flat package. Hmm. . . . This is promising, a new bird book perhaps," he mused. He pulled off the last bit of paper. "What on earth?"

It was an artist's coat—with at least a dozen colorful pockets.

He stared at it for a moment. Then slowly he smiled. "This is actually quite useful. It has plenty of room for my binoculars and my other belongings. I won't have to search for my keys and glasses all the time anymore. What a splendid present!"

31

32

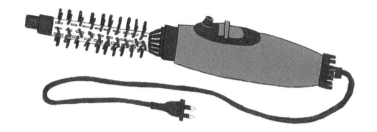

Mildred had just finished eating a healthy breakfast of granola and an apple. She tidied the kitchen right away, and then stepped over to her painting equipment. A large white canvas sat invitingly, waiting for the strokes of her paintbrush.

The new painting was already crystal clear in her mind. She flicked her long bangs out of her eyes and closed them.

"I see a wide, black line at the bottom and two thinner ones at the top. A flattened red ball between them."

There was a knock on the door—a package had arrived. Mildred decided to open the oblong package right away. Her work on the painting had already been interrupted anyway.

Mildred squinted at the gift in front of her. "What a peculiar choice from the Perkson family," she said, picking up the curling iron. "Well, I might as well try it on my bangs. Maybe that way I can keep them out of my eyes while I paint."

Thirty minutes later, Mildred stood gazing at her curly-haired image in the entrance hall mirror. She nodded to her own reflection, quite pleased with it.

C ousin Scott was moping in his room. He
grunted when his mother knocked on the
door. He didn't even thank her for the large
package and envelope that appeared on the
floor in front of him.

"I don't feel like opening that present," Scott
muttered. "The Perksons always get me baby-
ish stuff." He reached for the envelope. "I hope
there's money in here."

N o, there was no money in there. Instead, he found a gift certificate to the bird shop: Good for One Parrot.

Surprised, Scott looked at the package and unwrapped it. It was a large birdcage!

"Where are you rushing to now?" Scott's mother called as he stormed past her. But he didn't have time to answer. He was in a big hurry to get to the bird shop.

*How cool!* Scott thought. *A parrot of my own. None of my friends have one!*

Frustrated, Aunt Trudy stood in her hall next to a big box.

"How inconsiderate to send such a large present," she grumbled. "I have to go through such trouble opening it. And what am I supposed to do with all that cardboard and bubble wrap?"

The present turned out to be so surprising that for once Aunt Trudy was speechless. She reached into the box and picked out parts—to an electric drum set!

Soon the drum set stood ready in all its glory. All there was left to do was plug it in.

"Those Perksons guessed my secret dream!" Aunt Trudy said, amazed. "For seventy years I've been too embarrassed to tell anyone that I would love to play the drums."

Aunt Trudy put the headphones on and let loose. She played for the entire day. By evening, her normally tight shoulders were relaxed for once, and the wild rhythms had messed up her firmly curled bangs.

"What a wonderful gift," Trudy said. "I must call the Perksons right away and thank them."

Mom put the phone down. She was as red as a ripe tomato.

"You'll never guess what has happened," she said slowly. "Aunt Trudy accidentally got the drum set—and she's very happy about it!"

"Don't tell me Scott got Aunt Trudy's hair curler!" Alfie exclaimed.

A phone call to Scott's mother revealed the next switcheroo. Scott's mom said Scott had been sitting in his room the whole evening talking to his new parrot!

"Scott has even been laughing!" she reported.

Mom still looked upset.

"There's no reason to worry," Dad reassured her. "Both Trudy and Scott are thrilled with their gifts."

"I wonder what Mildred and Eddie will say about their presents," Mom murmured. She rubbed her head. "I'm getting a headache!"

Mom escaped to the couch and hid under a blanket. She wouldn't take the phone later, even though Mildred was calling to thank her for the curling iron.

Dad listened to Mildred's excited description of her new curly hairdo. "Mildred has decided to change the style of her paintings as well," he said. "She says the next piece will have wavy lines in it!"

"But there's still Uncle Eddie. I can't imagine him being delighted with the artist's coat," Mom moaned from under the blanket. "Please call him."

Fortunately, Mom was wrong. Uncle Eddie was strolling around happily in his coat with all the pockets. "I should've gotten a coat like this a long time ago," he told Dad on the phone. "I'll never lose my belongings again!"

He tapped the red pocket, where he had stowed his binoculars. As soon as he hung up with Dad, he was going to watch the birds at the feeder.

The day before Christmas Eve was difficult. Dad's outdoor Christmas lights had begun to flicker. Mom lay in bed with a cold towel on her forehead.

"This is not how I planned it," Mom groaned. "This was supposed to be a perfect Christmas!"

The children could see that their parents were getting very upset. "It's time for us to take over, Alfie," Ava said.

Alfie nodded. "Let's go!"

The children ran to the kitchen and rummaged in the cupboards and the fridge. There was enough food all right, but they didn't know how to prepare a Christmas dinner.

"I wish we knew how to make Christmas turkey," Alfie said. Ava decided to call Mildred and Aunt Trudy. Maybe one of them could help.

43

On Christmas morning, Alfie and Ava woke up early. They were excited to open their presents, but that would come a little bit later. First they needed to check on a few things.

From downstairs, they could already hear clattering noises. They sneaked past the parents' bedroom and into the kitchen. Their plan had worked perfectly. The mouth-watering smell of turkey filled the room.

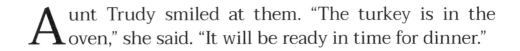

A unt Trudy smiled at them. "The turkey is in the oven," she said. "It will be ready in time for dinner."

"We baked buns, too," Mildred said, showing them a basket.

"What can we do to help?" Alfie asked.

Mildred and Aunt Trudy gave the children some quick instructions. Soon they were busy, too, peeling vegetables, polishing silverware, and setting the table.

Still in her nightgown, Mom tiptoed to the kitchen. She beamed when she saw the magic that her helpers had created.

46

That evening, after everyone had opened presents, and enjoyed the delicious Christmas dinner, the children asked everyone to gather in front of the window. They had a Christmas surprise: snow lanterns of different sizes illuminated the trees and bushes of the garden.

"How beautiful!" Mom said.

"Amazing!" Dad agreed, hugging them.

Mom started quietly singing a Christmas carol, and soon everyone joined in.

It didn't matter at all that Dad's Christmas lights were still flickering. It was another perfect Christmas at the Perksons' house.